MW00974927

# The Three Bears' Halloween

by KATHY DUVAL

illustrated by PAUL MEISEL

HOLIDAY HOUSE / New York

To Jon Paul, Jr., Madison, and Bethany,
who always amaze and delight me
K. D.

For Mom and Dad
P. M.

Text copyright © 2007 by Kathy Duval
Illustrations copyright © 2007 by Paul Meisel
All Rights Reserved
Printed in the United States of America
The artwork for this book was created with acrylic paints
and gouache on paper.
The text typeface is McKracken.
www.holidayhouse.com
First Edition
1 3 5 7 9 10 8 6 4 2

Library of Congress Cataloging-in-Publication Data
Duval, Kathy.
The Three Bears' Halloween / by Kathy Duval ; illustrated by Paul Meisel. – 1st ed.
p. cm.
Summary: Is it a witch or a blonde little girl hiding in the bushes of the spooky house
when the three bears go trick or treating?
ISBN-13: 978-0-8234-2032-2 (hardcover)
ISBN-10: 0-8234-2032-9 (hardcover)
[1. Halloween–Fiction. 2. Bears–Fiction.]
I. Meisel, Paul, ill. II. Title.
PZ7.D9547Thb 2007
[E]–dc22
2006012120

It was Halloween.

Papa Bear put on funny ears.
Mama Bear put on funny hair.
Baby Bear put on a mask with big, sharp teeth.
"Boo!" he shouted.

Mama and Papa Bear jumped. "You look scary!"
Baby Bear picked up a bag. "Let's go!"
The bears went trick-or-treating.

"Boo!" Baby Bear yelled down a hole.
A squirrel gave him nuts.

"Boo! Boo!" he shouted into a bush.
Some bees gave him honey.

"Boo! Boo! Boo!" he called up a tree.
A family of birds dropped berries in his bag.

"Look! I'm so scary, my trick-or-treat bag
is almost full!" said Baby Bear.
The bears saw a house covered with spiderwebs.
Baby Bear shivered. "Someone has a very scary house!"
Mama Bear clucked her tongue. "Someone is very messy!"

Baby Bear knocked on the door. "Trick or treat!" CREEEAK! The door swung open. No one was there.

"Someone must have forgotten
to shut the door," said Papa.

"TEE-HEE-HEE!"
"Someone's laughing!" said Papa.
"Someone's in the bushes!" said Mama.
"Someone wearing a tall, scary hat!"
said Baby Bear.

The bears hurried inside the house, and Papa shut the door.
"I smell something," said Mama.
"Something yummy!" said Papa.
"Scary popcorn spiders!" said Baby Bear.

Mama nibbled a licorice leg.
Papa nibbled two legs, and Baby Bear ate
a whole popcorn spider.

**"TEE-HEE-HEE!"**
"Someone's outside!" said Papa.
"Someone's peeking in the window!" said Mama.
"Someone with a scary broom!" said Baby Bear.

The bears ran into the living room.
Baby Bear tripped over a chair and broke it to bits.
The bears jumped behind the couch.

CREEEAK!
"Someone's opening the door!" said Papa.
"Someone's in the kitchen!" said Mama.
"Someone with a big, scary nose," said Baby Bear.

The bears ran upstairs, dived into bed,

and pulled the covers over their heads.

# "TEE-HEE-HEE!"
"Someone's creeping up the stairs!" whispered Papa.

"TEE-HEE-HEE!"
"Someone's tiptoeing in the bedroom!" whispered Mama.

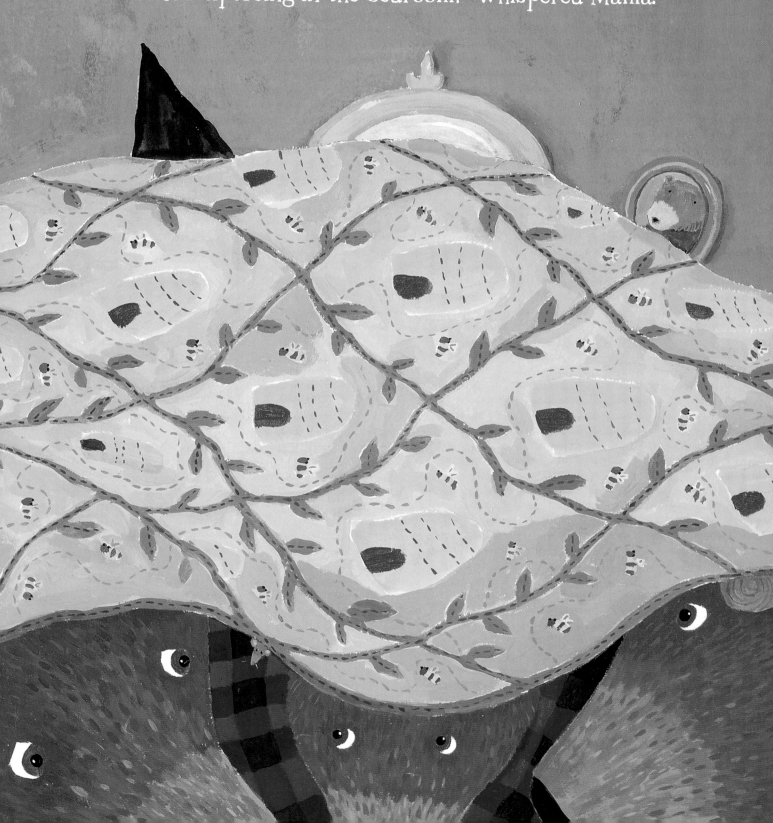

"TEE-HEE-HEE!"
Baby Bear peeked over the covers.
"Someone is a Big, Bad Witch!" he yelled. "Run!"

Papa, Mama, and Baby Bear leaped out of bed.

They ran down the stairs,
across the living room,
through the kitchen,
and out the door.